hen

star

cup

pup

YOKO Learns to Read

ROSEMARY WELLS

Disney · HYPERION BOOKS

NEW YORK

しあわせのにんぎょう

ほしのおひめさま

みっつのきんのたまご

Yoko and her mama loved to read their three books
from Japan.
Yoko knew *The Happy Doll*, *The Star Princess*, and
Three Golden Eggs by heart.

At school, Mrs. Jenkins gave Yoko three leaves, one for each book.
Proudly, Yoko pinned her leaves on the class book tree.
Yoko noticed that Valerie had four leaves,

and Angelo had six leaves.
Olive and Sylvia, between them, had nine leaves.
Yoko had no other books at home.

That night, Yoko would not eat her favorite sushi.

"I am stuck at three book leaves," said Yoko to Mama.

"Olive and Sylvia said I would be left behind."

"Let's read *The Golden Eggs*, or maybe *The Star Princess!*"
said Yoko's mama.

"No, Mama," said Yoko. "I already have those book leaves."

Yoko's mama went to school to see Mrs. Jenkins.

"Yoko is afraid to be left behind," said Yoko's mama.

Mrs. Jenkins said, "Oh, but you can make all the difference!

Just read one book out loud with Yoko every night!"
Yoko's mama did not tell Mrs. Jenkins that she herself
could not read even one word on the classroom wall.

Yoko and her mama put on their best kimonos
for their trip to the library.
Yoko got her own library card with her name on it.
She picked out a beautiful book about a fox.

Mr. Chatterjee, the librarian, stamped it and handed it to Yoko.
"Bring the book back when you finish it. Then you may choose
a different one," said Mr. Chatterjee.
"I can't wait to read it!" said Yoko.

 At home Yoko and her mama sat at their tea table.
Yoko's mama turned the pages from the back to the front.
"In English books, we turn the pages the other way,
Mama," said Yoko. "I learned that in school!"

Yoko and her mama followed the story by looking at the pictures.
Yoko pointed to the cover. "I have seen these three words before.
They are on Mrs. Jenkins's word wall!
Tomorrow I will find out what they are."

In school, Yoko copied the words onto a new book leaf.

Then she told the picture story out loud.

Mrs. Jenkins put the fourth book leaf up on the tree.

"Telling isn't reading!" Olive and Sylvia whispered.

"I think you can read these words, Yoko," said Mrs. Jenkins.
She pointed to **the**, **red**, and **fox** on the word wall.
"Words are like faces," said Mrs. Jenkins. "Easy to remember!"
"Now that I know *The Red Fox*, I need another book!" said Yoko.

On the way to the library, Yoko saw a sign.

"Look, Mama!" she said. "It says **BUS STOP**!"

"I am so proud of my little snow flower," said Yoko's mama.

Yoko's new book was about a bunny who could fly.
The bunny was wearing colorful shoes.
"**Shhh**," said Yoko. "I'll bet
that **SH** word is **SHOES**! It just makes sense!"

On the school bus, Yoko showed her book to Maggie.
Maggie was in second grade and could read.
"**Magic** has a soft **g** like **gym** and a hard **c** like **cup**," she said.
"Now I will get my fifth book leaf!" said Yoko.

Yoko and her mama brought *The Magic Shoes* back to Mr. Chatterjee.
He suggested *Snug as a Bug in a Rug* for Yoko.
On their way out, Yoko read the word on the door for her mama.
"**LIBRARY**!" said Yoko. "It just makes sense!"

Yoko had no trouble finishing *Snug as a Bug in a Rug*.
Mrs. Jenkins awarded Yoko her sixth book leaf.

"I bet you can't read my book!" said Sylvia the next day.

"Or my book!" said Olive.

Yoko took a deep breath, then let it out.

"*Sam's Pink Pig!*" she said, and "*My Big Bad Hat.*"

Yoko could not wait to tell her mama.
"Olive and Sylvia didn't believe me!" said Yoko.
"But they found out, Mama. I can read!
I can really, really read!"

Outside, the night wind blew and the snow flew.
Inside, Yoko and her mama read their books.
"Do you think I could learn to read in English, too?"
asked Yoko's mama.

Yoko took out her crayon and paper and made a shape.

"What is that?" asked Yoko's mama.

"It's an **A**," said Yoko. "That's where we start!"

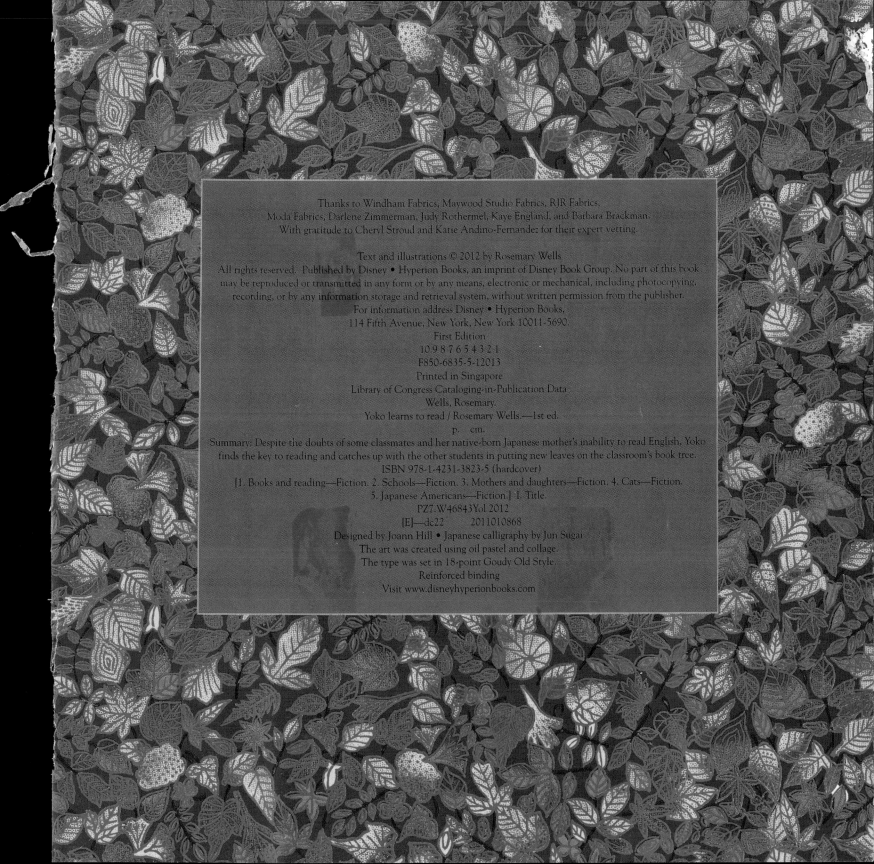

Thanks to Windham Fabrics, Maywood Studio Fabrics, RJR Fabrics,
Moda Fabrics, Darlene Zimmerman, Judy Rothermel, Kaye England, and Barbara Brackman.
With gratitude to Cheryl Stroud and Katie Andino-Fernandez for their expert vetting.

First Edition
10 9 8 7 6 5 4 3 2 1
F850-6835-5-12013
Printed in Singapore
Library of Congress Cataloging-in-Publication Data
Wells, Rosemary.
Yoko learns to read / Rosemary Wells.—1st ed.
p.   cm.
Summary: Despite the doubts of some classmates and her native-born Japanese mother's inability to read English, Yoko
finds the key to reading and catches up with the other students in putting new leaves on the classroom's book tree.
ISBN 978-1-4231-3823-5 (hardcover)
[1. Books and reading—Fiction. 2. Schools—Fiction. 3. Mothers and daughters—Fiction. 4. Cats—Fiction.
5. Japanese Americans—Fiction.] I. Title.
PZ7.W46843Yol 2012
[E]—dc22   2011010868
Designed by Joann Hill • Japanese calligraphy by Jun Sugai
The art was created using oil pastel and collage.
The type was set in 18-point Goudy Old Style.
Reinforced binding
Visit www.disneyhyperionbooks.com

bat

hat

top

cat